Wishes *can* come true . . . if you know what to do!

It was then that Berry suddenly noticed her right eye was blinking. Was there a speck in it, or was it just embarrassment?

Better say something before anybody remembers the horrible mistake with the camera, thought Berry. So, as she scratched her left knee and blinked her right eye, Berry said the first thing that popped into her mind. "What I *really* wish I had more than anything in the world is a video camera," she said.

The miracle had begun.

SCRAMBLED EGGS

ALMOST STARRING DAD

Suzanne Allen

Illustrated by Cornelius Van Wright

SPLASH™

A BERKLEY / SPLASH BOOK

SCRAMBLED EGGS

ALMOST STARRING DAD

Chapter One

For the first eight years of her life, Beryllium Turner had walked into video rental stores with her head held high. Now, at age nine, Berry had to sneak into Video World at the Prospect Park Mall in San Diego. Sneaking along right behind Berry was her almost-twin stepsister, Terri.

Mrs. Lily Turner knew all about Berry and Terri sneaking into Video World. She was Berry's real mother and owned Books & Bears, a book and toy store next to Video World. Mrs. Turner liked to watch video movies herself. Lolling on the old couch in the den and watching video movies was once a favorite sloppy habit of Lily Sterling and her family. But no more.

Things had changed a lot since Lily Sterling married Nicholas Turner. Berry Sterling got a new last name. She already had one older brother and two older sisters. Berry had thought *that* was too many. Now she also had a new older brother and a new older sister, plus something she'd never had before:

a *younger* sister. It was true that Terri was only three *days* younger. But once the Turners had moved in, Berry was no longer the youngest in the family.

Seven kids in one family was a lot. Berry thought it was too many. The old Sterling house was big, but it was not *that* big. When the Turners moved in, Berry got stuck sharing a room with Terri.

Miss Messy and Miss Prissy did not fit well together at first. Was there a room in the world large enough to hold all Berry's junk and all Terri's tidiness? At first, it didn't seem so.

But now things were slowly improving. Clutterbug Berry was finally getting used to sharing a room with Neat Freak Terri.

Neither of them was used to sneaking into Video World, though. "Hurry!" whispered Terri, crowding Berry into the store ahead of her.

"Relax, for goodness sake! Dad isn't anywhere around!" said Berry. She stumbled through the turnstile inside the door, pushed from behind by Terri.

"You never can tell," said Terri. She didn't stop prodding at her stepsister until they were hidden behind one of the long racks that displayed videotapes for rent.

Terri was right. You couldn't always tell where Mr. Turner would be. He was supposed to be working in the new six-plex cinema he owned—Movies, Movies, Movies. It was right down at the other end of the mall.

But Mr. Turner liked to take a break now and then. Then he would wander down the mall to visit his wife in *her* store. To do that, he had to walk right past Video World. Mr. Turner hated Video World.

Mr. Turner usually stopped, shaded his eyes, and peered through the glass windows of Video World. Berry had seen him do it several times. His face was always grim. Maybe he was counting the dollars that were going into the cash registers at Video World instead of Movies, Movies, Movies.

Whatever he was doing, Mr. Turner's little habit of stopping and staring made Video World a dangerous place for Berry and Terri. " 'Course he hasn't exactly *forbidden* us to be in here," said Berry as Terri started for the children's section, her head low. Despite Berry's words, she kept her head down, too. Mr. Turner was a quiet man, but he was very stern.

"Every dollar that goes to Video World to rent a movie is a dollar out of my pocket," they had heard Mr. Turner say many times. So on the day that

Movies, Movies, Movies opened, the family had given Mr. Turner a little present. Berry, Terri, and the rest of the family all promised not to rent movies on videotape for a whole year. That was the family's way of saying that they were standing right behind their dad, helping his new cinemas to succeed.

It had seemed like such a good idea at the time. Now, as Berry gazed longingly at the brightly colored boxes, she wished they had given up videotape movies for a slightly shorter time. Say . . . three weeks?

Yes, three weeks sounded right. Long enough for everybody to feel really good about doing it. But not so long as to miss some great new movies that were out on videotape.

Berry watched enviously as people around her chose movies and took them to the front counter. Meanwhile, Terri had a box in each hand. She wished more than anything she could take them home with her. The boxes were two different feature-length cartoons she had never seen before.

The girls were so distracted that for a moment neither noticed a familiar figure loom against the glass of the front window. "Oh, no! There he is!" said Terri. She ducked behind a large cardboard ad-

4

vertising display standing on the floor. Berry quickly joined her. Had they been spotted?

Fortunately, Video World was huge, one of a chain of stores dotted across San Diego. The children's section was way in the back of the store. As usual, Mr. Turner was more interested in scowling at customers near the checkout counter, which was right up front.

"I hope Mom doesn't squeal on us," whispered Berry, peeking at the shadow in the window. Terri, meanwhile, was reading the large cardboard display she was crouching behind.

Why rent movies from Video World?
Well, you tell us! On videotape!
VIDEO WORLD'S SECOND ANNUAL
TV-COMMERCIAL CONTEST!

"Fabulous prizes for the best homemade TV commercial telling why people should rent from Video World," whispered Terri over her shoulder to Berry.

"What fabulous prizes?" whispered Berry.

Terri was silent a moment, reading further. "For the under-thirteen age group, first prize is two free movie rentals a week for a whole year." Suddenly

Terri gave a loud laugh. Then she slapped her hand over her mouth.

Berry peeked around the rack of videotapes toward the window. "You can keep on laughing. He's gone," she said in a normal voice. "But what was so funny, anyway?"

"You'd have to know my dad a little better," said Terri, looking embarrassed. For a moment, Berry thought Terri wasn't going to explain.

Finally Terri said, "Well, he's a not a cheapskate or anything. But he really loves bargains. If it's free, he goes crazy! I suddenly thought, well, he wouldn't know what to do with *free* movies on videotape. He'd almost *have* to watch them. Boy, I *wish* we could win this contest!"

Berry looked at Terri in amazement. It was the taller, slimmer Terri who was always so sensible. Terri got things done. She didn't waste her time with silly ideas.

Berry was shorter, freckled, and, thank goodness, three days older. She was the one who had all the foolish fantasies that never quite worked out. But now Terri had *wished* for something—something as silly and impossible as winning a TV-commercial contest! Berry was seeing a whole new stepsister!

Berry felt a warm glow of friendship. She shoul-

7

dered in beside Terri to study the sign. She might as well share this little fantasy. There might never be another chance like this.

"Boy! Look at the grand prize!" said Berry. "A twelve-hundred-dollar videotape camera. Wouldn't *that* be neat?"

"Mm," said Terri, a faraway smile on her face. "I wouldn't mind making TV commercials when I grow up."

"Me, either," said Berry. "Of course, there *is* a problem." There was *always* a problem. And it was always too big to solve. Berry was wise in the ways of fantasies.

"I know. The grand prize can be won by kids right up to the age of seventeen," said Terri. "We wouldn't have a chance."

"That's not what I meant. It's a chicken-and-egg thing," said Berry.

"A what?" said Terri.

"You know. Which came first, the chicken or the egg? You need the camera to make the commercial to win the camera to make the commercial." She spun her finger in circles.

Terri frowned. It was indeed a problem. A big problem. The Turners did not own a video camera.

An impossible problem, thought Berry. The *usual*

8

kind of problem. Which was why fantasies were just that, fantasies, dreams that never came true. Berry thought she knew all there was to know about fantasies.

But she didn't.

Chapter Two

A miracle happened that night at the supper table. It was so astounding that Berry remembered long afterward what she was doing at the very moment it happened.

Berry had a fleck of something in her right eye, and was blinking furiously. The fleck had come right in the middle of a terrible itching on her left kneecap. So Berry quite clearly remembered that she was blinking with her right eye and scratching with her left hand when the miracle happened.

The miracle didn't happen right away. It crept up on everybody quite slowly. There were several things that caused it. The first was the main course at supper.

"We'll have loud cheers for the housekeeper," announced Dorothea in her funny Australian accent as she passed warm plates around the table.

"Why?" asked everybody.

"Cheers first," insisted Dorothea as she went back into the kitchen. Everybody cheered. The true

Turners and the former Sterlings were all scrambled together around the table. You had to listen very closely to hear two very different types of cheers.

There were loud, messy cheers that ended in squeaks and roars and rattles of breath. Those were Sterling-Turner cheers. With all the table-thumping and rattling, they sounded like vacuum cleaners falling downstairs.

There were also small, well-behaved cheers that had tidy beginnings and careful, rounded endings. Those were true Turner cheers. They were clipped as neatly as hedges.

These days, though, you had to look or listen closely to notice where the true Turners began and the Sterling-Turners left off. They were really becoming one big, happy family.

"Thank you, thank you! It's everybody's favorite—spaghetti!" said Dorothea as she returned with a huge, steaming bowl. Everybody had a really good reason to cheer now. They all cheered again.

How could spaghetti cause a miracle? Well, spaghetti was one dish that quite unscrambled the scrambled-together Turners. On a spaghetti night, anyone could spot the members of the two families.

12

First, there were the former Sterlings, led by Mrs. Turner herself.

Her daughter Vanessa, aged sixteen, was the cheeriest of all the kids. Vanessa greeted her spaghetti like a long-lost friend. But since she greeted almost everybody and everything that way, the spaghetti had no reason to feel special.

Tristan was fourteen. He had the wild hair and eyes of a mad scientist ready to perform horrible experiments on his plateful of noodles.

Thanks to hair sprayed in several hideous shades, twelve-year-old Isabella was the most noticeable of all the kids. Everybody did notice Izzy. They noticed that they could hardly see her behind the huge mountain of spaghetti she had heaped on her plate.

Finally there was Berry, who liked spaghetti so much she had once dreamed she was a meatball.

These five Sterling-Turners all ate spaghetti in exactly the same way. They forked huge haystacks of spaghetti into their mouths and bit off the trailing ends, allowing them to fall back onto the plate.

The true Turners, headed by Mr. Turner, ate their spaghetti very differently.

Paul, aged fifteen, loved spaghetti because he loved to solve problems. How to get spaghetti neatly onto a fork? Paul's spaghetti grew cold as he wrestled happily with all the loose ends.

Thirteen-year-old Melissa, the prissiest of all the Turners, was going to be a fashion model one day. Spaghetti was her greatest challenge. She knew that anybody who could eat spaghetti while looking stylish and beautiful was going right to the top of the fashion world.

And then there was Terri Turner, aged nine and only three days younger than her stepsister Berry. Terri had positively *hated* spaghetti all her life. Being a true Turner, she was far too well-mannered to let anyone know it.

The true Turners all ate spaghetti in exactly the same way. They did not bend over their plates with spaghetti sauce dribbling down their chins. They sat upright and twiddled and twiddled with a fork and a spoon until each strand of spaghetti was twirled into a neat little spool.

"*We* eat spaghetti like real Italians do it," said Berry Sterling-Turner as she bit off another haystack.

"*We* eat spaghetti like real *polite* Italians do it," said Terri Turner-Turner. She popped a perfectly twirled forkful into her mouth and tried not to wrinkle her nose.

"Grammar, Terri, grammar," said Mrs. Turner cheerfully. "That's 'really polite.' Not 'real polite.' " Then she, too, was silent as she popped a haystack into her mouth and bit off the ends. Terri looked at Mrs. Turner and could hardly believe her eyes. How could somebody be so tidy with words, and so untidy with food?

Thanks to spaghetti, the true Turners couldn't help noticing the Sterling-Turners, and vice versa. The miracle was beginning to brew.

The next cause of the miracle was the subject of conversation at the table. It came up when Mr. Turner announced that his new cinemas had done better than expected in their first two months. There were more cheers around the table. Mr. Turner beamed proudly.

"You must be very pleased, dear," said Mrs. Turner.

"Yes, I am," said Mr. Turner. "As you know, I've always wanted to own my own cinema instead of managing one for somebody else."

What have *you* always wanted to do with your life? It was a subject that led directly to the miracle.

The true Turners thought it was an important subject and always discussed it seriously. Izzy Turner (an ex-Sterling, remember) said she always wanted to be a rock star. She was surprised and pleased when the true Turners thought about it very carefully.

"A hard choice, Izzy," said Mr. Turner. "I understand that successful rock stars have to work and work to be any good."

"But they *can* make a lot of money," said Paul, as serious as his father.

"What will you call yourself, Izzy?" asked Terri Turner politely. That was the last sensible thing anybody said for a while.

The trouble was, the Sterling-Turners were *never* serious about this kind of dinner-table conversation. They saw it as a chance for good-natured teasing. Strange names for a rock star and her backup band began to fly around the table.

"Izzy Real!"

"Izzy Dead and the Corpses!"

"Izzy Fizzy and the Warm Pop Bottles!"

Izzy stuck out her tongue at her mother and her real brother and sisters. Mr. Turner reached over and patted her on the hand. "There, there, Izzy. You get rich. Show us all," he said with a kindly smile.

Now the miracle was almost upon them.

There was a small moment when not one of the

many mouths around the table was talking. Berry and Terri both knew how hard it was for a nine-year-old to get a word in edgeways.

Foolishly, Berry jumped into the silence with the first words that came into her head. "*I've* always wanted to make TV commercials," she said. Already, she was scratching her left knee. That's how close things were to a miracle.

Almost as soon as the words were out of her mouth, Berry wondered why she had spoken. She glanced around at her real brother and sisters. What a mistake she had made! She was going to get teased, for sure.

But Mr. Turner spoke first, and again he was serious. "An interesting career, Berry," he said. "Do you want to produce commercials, or direct them, or just be a cameraman?"

Berry knew what a cameraman did, but that was all. "A cameraman," she said. Mr. Turner nodded. It seemed a reasonable answer to him.

So far so good, thought Berry. Then she remembered the day last summer when she had borrowed her mother's tiny pocket camera. Somehow Berry had looked through the wrong hole while she was clicking the shutter. Instead of wonderful photos of

17

family fun on the beach, Berry had taken twelve dark, fuzzy pictures of her right eyeball.

It was then that Berry suddenly noticed her right eye was blinking. Was there a speck in it, or was it just embarrassment?

Better say something before anybody remembers the horrible mistake with the camera, thought Berry. So, as she scratched her left knee and blinked her right eye, Berry said the first thing that popped into her mind. "What I *really* wish I had more than anything in the world is a video camera," she said.

The miracle had begun.

Chapter Three

Berry expected support from Mr. Turner. But he was silent. Her words had not impressed him. He had come to expect that type of hopeless, wishy-washy thinking from his stepchildren. Why work for things when you can wish for them? Thank goodness my own children don't think that way, he thought.

But the next words spoken at the table stabbed him right to the heart. "Boy, I wish we had a video camera, too!" said Terri.

Mr. Turner turned in astonishment. His own true daughter had betrayed him! After all his lectures on the importance of hard work! "Terri, I'm shocked," said Mr. Turner sternly.

"In fact, I'm shocked at both of you," he continued. "There are doers in this world, and there are dreamers. I'd hate to think that my two youngest daughters will be dreamers. People get places by good, hard work, not by lazing around and saying, 'I wish, I wish.'"

Terri lowered her eyes. She knew how her father felt about such things. Why had she opened her mouth?

Berry was shocked. She'd been wishing for things out loud for most of her life. Suddenly it seemed the wrong thing to do. Her cheeks began to burn.

"I didn't become the owner of Movies, Movies, Movies by wishing for it," continued Mr. Turner. "I had to work hard for years. Your mother and I didn't have things as easy as you do today. When I was growing up, I had to walk five miles to school. . . ." Blah, blah, blah . . . Mr. Turner went on and on.

Everybody else around the table began to pick at their food and feel sorry for Berry and Terri. The two girls, already the smallest members of the family, both felt smaller and smaller.

Their housekeeper was the first to become impatient with Mr. Turner's long lecture. Dorothea started to clear away the plates. She banged them together noisily, as waitresses in restaurants sometimes do when it's past closing time and they want to get rid of slow eaters.

But Mr. Turner was talking about one of his most favorite subjects in the whole world—the value of hard work. He didn't notice the angry dish-banging. There was no stopping him.

At the other end of the table, Mrs. Turner began to look a little grim herself. Surely *everyone* needed to dream a little! she thought.

Indeed, Mrs. Turner had dreamed about getting married again after her first husband died. When you looked at it that way, Nicholas Turner was Lily Turner's dream come true. No, her husband was carrying things too far. Berry and Terri didn't deserve this.

"I'm sure you've all heard about the ant who worked all summer while the grasshopper played," said Mr. Turner. "You know what happened to the foolish grasshopper when winter came."

"Yes!" interrupted all the true Turners quickly. They had heard their father tell this story many times. They did not want to hear it again.

"Does everyone know the story?" asked Mr. Turner. He loved to tell about how the hard-working ant survived the cold winter while the lazy grasshopper shivered. He thought perhaps the Sterling-Turners would like to hear the fable.

"Yes!" chorused the Sterling-Turners. Actually, what most of them really said was "Ow—yes!" This was because they were all being kicked under the table by the Turner children. The true Turners wanted to make *sure* they didn't have to hear the story again.

Mr. Turner seemed a little disappointed. "Well, then I won't repeat the story." All the true Turners gave little sighs of relief. "But the moral of the story is important. . . ." Blah, blah, blah . . . Mr. Turner still had lots to say on the subject of laziness and wishful thinking.

Oh, this is too much! thought Mrs. Turner. Besides, if I don't do something soon Dorothea's going to start breaking all my dishes, she's banging them so hard in the kitchen.

Mrs. Turner made a sudden decision. The last part of the miracle fell into place.

"I've got to go and fetch something," she said, standing and interrupting Mr. Turner. She was back a few moments later, a large cardboard box in her arms. Mr. Turner was still droning on and on about hard workers who succeeded and good-for-nothings who failed.

"Excuse me, dear. I have a little something here for our own pair of grasshoppers," said Mrs. Turner. "Berry and Terri, I know it's nowhere near your birthdays, but, well, you're getting your present a little early this year. Sorry I didn't have time to wrap it."

"Couldn't this wait?" said Mr. Turner.

"No, I don't think so, dear," said Mrs. Turner brightly. "You see, Berry and Terri, your wish has come true. It *does* happen now and then, I'm pleased to say. I'm giving you a video camera."

"A *what?*" said Mr. Turner.

There was a shout from the kitchen. "Hey, now! Let's hear it for the grasshoppers!" Then Dorothea laughed loudly. At least, it sounded loud. That's because everyone else was sitting around the table in stunned silence.

Berry was no longer blinking or scratching. She was pinching herself. She couldn't believe that after a lifetime of wishing great big hopeless wishes, one of those wishes had actually come true!

Chapter Four

The family living room was pandemonium. In the center of the floor, Berry and Terri were sitting and peeling away layers of cardboard and Styrofoam. Mrs. Turner was sitting on the couch with her arms crossed, enjoying the unwrapping of the video camera.

Mr. Turner had come to watch, too. He was sitting in a chair and he seemed calm. But his own kids kept glancing at him. They knew their father must be seething inside. They still couldn't believe their stepmother had done such a thing to him.

"It isn't fair!" cried Tristan.

"Why did *they* get it?" asked Paul.

"Because they wished for it first," said Mrs. Turner calmly.

All the older Turner kids eyed one another.

"I wish for a personal computer with a hard-disk drive," said Paul suddenly.

"I wish for my own car," said Vanessa.

"An electric guitar!" "A sailboat!" "A modeling course!" all the others chimed in.

"Well?" said Izzy after a moment of silence.

"Sorry," said Mrs. Turner with a shrug. "I don't have any of those things." Berry, listening with half an ear, smiled to herself. She knew exactly what her brothers and sisters were doing wrong. They had to scratch their left knee and blink their right eye while they were wishing!

"But why should *they* get something that's so expensive?" wailed Izzy.

"The camera's worth thousands of dollars," agreed Melissa.

"Only a thousand or so, actually," said Mrs. Turner.

"Well, I expect to get something for my birthday that costs *just* as much!" said Izzy fiercely.

"I'll make a note of that, Izzy," said Mrs. Turner. "Since the video camera cost me exactly nothing, I'll be sure to spend the same amount on your present."

"Wait a minute!" "How?" "What!" "It isn't fair!" The cries came thick and fast.

At last Mrs. Turner held up her hand and said, "If you'll all stop talking and listen for a moment, I'll explain. You, too, Berry and Terri."

"If you remember, last Christmas the Prospect Park Mall Tenants' Association held a Christmas decoration contest. Thanks to lots of helping hands, my store won first prize," said Mrs. Turner.

Everyone remembered. "It was a dumb plaque to put up on the wall," said Vanessa.

"That's just what I thought, too," said Mrs. Turner. "Well, we were both wrong. The real prize was this video camera. I must have missed the meeting before Christmas when they decided to give a prize. I didn't know about it until it showed up one day in the spring. I'm afraid the Tenants' Association isn't very organized."

"Well, lots of us helped win it," said Tristan. "So how come we're all not sharing the camera?"

"Why, I'm sure you will," said Mrs. Turner. "You'll share the camera with your brothers and sisters, won't you, Berry and Terri?" Her words sounded just a little bit more like an order than a question.

"Sure. You can use it anytime we don't want it," agreed Berry generously.

"But only as long as you're all very careful," added Terri sternly.

"But I don't see why *they*—!" said Izzy angrily.

Her mother interrupted her. "I want all of you

27

to use it. And I did think of giving it to all of you. But then I wondered, would Berry and Terri ever get to use it?"

"Of course!" said Paul.

"Yeah!" said Izzy.

"Ha!" said Terri.

"Fat chance!" said Berry.

"I'm afraid the way things work around here, I have to agree with Berry and Terri," said Mrs. Turner. "You older children would never let Berry and Terri near the camera."

Mrs. Turner didn't say that she had first considered giving it to Mr. Turner. But Mr. Turner wanted everybody to get a pilot's license just to fly the family toaster. Giving it to her husband would mean *nobody* in the family would ever be allowed to use it.

"I'm sorry, everybody," said Mrs. Turner firmly. "This is one way to be certain *everybody* gets a chance to use the camera. So today is one of those rare days when the grasshoppers win, and everybody else loses. I don't want to hear any more about it."

The groans and moans that followed were music to the ears of Berry and Terri. Even Mrs. Turner's final words couldn't ruin their evening.

"Anyway, there'll be no playing with the camera this evening," she said. "You can all help Dorothea with the dishes. Then Berry and Terri will have lots of time to read the manual. They must do that before they get started."

That night at bedtime Berry and Terri went to find Mr. Turner. Terri gave her father a big hug. "I did listen to you at dinner, Dad," said Terri. "I promise I'll never wish for anything again." Not out loud at the dinner table, anyway, she thought to herself.

"It's all my fault," said Berry, taking her turn to hug her stepfather. "I'm the one who does all the wishing, really. Terri's really good at *doing* things, too. I'm glad I've got Terri for a sister."

Mr. Turner laughed. "It's nice of you to be loyal to Terri, but I'm not mad at her. Nor at you, Berry. I'm afraid I got a little carried away at the dinner table, that's all. I'm sorry."

Berry nodded seriously. "We forgive you," she said.

"So you're not mad at anybody?" asked Terri.

"Well, perhaps I am with your mother. Just a little. She embarrassed me in front of all of you. The same way I was embarrassing you. Nobody likes to be embarrassed in public, do they, little grasshoppers?"

"No," agreed Berry.

"But you've recovered, and so will I," said Mr. Turner, giving his daughter and stepdaughter fond good-night kisses.

"Don't worry, Dad," said Terri as they left. "We won't just play around with the camera like grasshoppers. We'll be real ants and do something great with it, I promise."

One manual and two beds meant that Berry and Terri were forced to share a bed. They both got into Terri's because half the stuffed toys in the universe were jammed into Berry's bed.

"Crazy, isn't it?" said Terri. "This afternoon we saw a contest. All we did was say 'I wish!' We won the grand prize without even doing *anything!*"

"Yeah!" said Berry happily. "So now we don't have to make a dumb TV commercial. We can just have fun with the camera, right?"

Terri was silent.

"Right?" said Berry.

"Well . . . I *did* tell Dad we'd do more than just play with it, remember?"

"*You* said that, I didn't," said Berry.

"Making a TV commercial would be *doing* something. And it would be fun, too," said Terri.

"Well . . . I don't know about the fun part," said Berry. "And anyway, what's the point? We can't win anything more. We've got the grand prize."

"Aren't you forgetting the first prize for under-thirteens?" said Terri. "Two movie rentals a week for fifty-two weeks."

"Gosh, that's right. I had forgotten," admitted Berry. "That *is* a good reason for making a TV commercial."

"Good. Let's do it then," said Terri. She was pleased with herself. It was hard to win an argument with Berry.

"At least, if you're *sure* we'd be allowed to watch them," said Berry.

"Dad won't be able to resist if they're free," promised Terri. She certainly hoped she was right.

Their plans made, the two of them lay for a while and stared at the shiny black camera. It was sitting on Tristan's tripod in the corner of the room.

"We're going to have trouble with Tris," said Berry at last.

"I know," said Terri. "He's being too nice, isn't he? Lending us his tripod and everything."

"He's trying to get the camera away from us, you know."

"Well, we won't let him get it, that's all," said Terri, opening the manual. The two settled down to read. They hardly quarreled at all about when to turn the page.

Finally Terri fell asleep. She dreamt she was accepting first prize in a TV-commercial contest.

Berry crept back to her own bed. Before she turned out the lights, she pulled out her diary from underneath the mattress and wrote:

Ma chère Annamarie,

My only true twin, guess what! There really is magic. If you know what to do, you really can wish for things and have them come true. And you don't have to use bats' tongues, or toads' warts, or anything. I'm not going to write down exactly how you do it, in case anyone reads this. But I can let you know it has something to do with scratching and blinking while you make a wish.

It has been nine years since we were separated by accident at the hospital. Now I am wishing that at last we will be reunited, and I

<u>am doing the secret things that make the wish</u>
<u>come true!</u>

See you in a day or so! By the way, if you want to be met at the airport, try to let us know what flight you are taking. I can't ask my mom to meet every plane from Paris, France.

Your true twin and loving step-triplet,
Beryllium

Chapter Five

Berry and Terri intended to start their TV commercial the very next day after school. Using the camera was not quite as easy as they had thought, however.

They loaded the battery pack and a videotape into the camera, then took turns operating it while the other read from the user's manual. Tristan hung about like a housefly. He was friendly, but he kept trying to fill their heads with unimportant things.

"It's the television director who yells 'roll camera' and 'cut' and tells the cameraman what to shoot at," said Tristan.

"Go away, Tristan," said Berry. Today they needed a cameraman and a manual-reader, not a director.

To begin with, they pressed the trigger of the camera for a few seconds, then removed the videocassette. They ran to the VCR under the television in the den and inserted the cassette. After a great deal of fast-forwarding and rewinding, they finally found a tiny little squirt of home video.

"There! I know what that is! It's the—" Too late. Whatever it was, it had flashed before their eyes on the television set and was gone. Several times the same thing happened. Gradually, they learned to take longer shots.

But the longer the shots, the more they realized that they moved the camera too quickly. Jerk! Slash! Swoop! The results were dizzying.

The zoom buttons were fun, too. They zoomed in and out, in *and* out, in AND out, until they were both seasick.

Naturally, they didn't want to accept too many favors from Tristan. So they did their best not to use his tripod. Unfortunately, everything they shot without it wobbled, sometimes a little (in Terri's hands) and sometimes a lot (in Berry's).

Finally they put the camera back on the tripod. Their videotaping began to look really professional. They made a rock-steady home video of the kitchen that was five minutes long.

"What are we going to call it? 'Butter Goes Moldy?' Nothing's moving," said Berry after three minutes.

"You're wrong, Berry," said Terri. "You can see the second hand moving on the kitchen clock."

But after watching all five minutes they both were bored. "We need action," said Berry.

Their next video was an animal video. It was rock-steady again, thanks to Tristan's tripod. They sneaked up on Kablooey, twenty-five pounds of furry yellow-and-white cat fat. She was lying on her back near the edge of the front porch, asleep in the late-afternoon sun. She became the star of another excellent five-minute video.

"Look! She's breathing! That's action!" said Terri as they viewed the results on the TV.

"Watch this zoom!" said Berry. Berry had indeed zoomed in. And in. The last two minutes looked like a rug heaving up and down on a waterbed.

At the very end of the video, Berry zoomed out just in time to catch Kablooey opening her eyes and giving a huge yawn. "I was *so* lucky to catch it. Isn't it a perfect yawn?" said Berry. She looked at Terri, who was yawning herself.

"We'll need to do something more interesting than this if we want to win a TV-commercial contest," said Terri.

People were more interesting. They were also harder to videotape. "Wait, wait!" cried Berry as

37

Terri struggled to set up the tripod. Too late. Vanessa had walked out of the room.

They chased Vanessa all over the house and found she was camera-shy. When they finally caught up with her in her room, she kept hiding her face behind a book and shouting, "Take that stupid thing away!"

They took the camera off the tripod again. That helped them keep up with their housekeeper as she cut the front grass.

"Presenting ... 'Dorothea Mows the Lawn,' " said Berry, waving to the television where their latest excellent video was about to begin. Wobble, wobble, wobble went the picture. Dorothea smiled at the camera.

Then she changed directions unexpectedly. The TV screen was empty. Swoosh! Swoop! Wobble! There she was again, still smiling. Oops. Gone again. Jerk! Wobble! Found again.

"I'm getting a headache," said Terri.

Tristan poked his head in the door of the den. "Can I see what you're doing?" he asked.

"No!" said Berry and Terri.

"Are you finished with the camera yet?"

"No!" said Berry and Terri. They shut the door to the den and pushed a chair against it, to keep him out. Then, one by one, they watched all their videotapes again.

Videotaping was definitely fun. But they had to admit their work did not deserve first prize for anything. Pointing the camera and pressing the trigger without any plan produced . . .

"Junk," said Berry with a sigh. Terri agreed with her. Winning a TV-commercial contest was not going to be easy. They needed a plan.

Tristan already had a plan. Just as they had feared, he was after the camera. When the two girls came to the dinner table, he was waiting for them.

"About time! Everybody agrees that it's someone else's turn to use the camera," said Tristan.

"Oh, no, you don't," said Berry angrily. She carefully set the camera on the tripod close to her chair, where she could reach it quickly if Tristan got grabby. "It's *our* camera, and we're *doing* something with it."

"But we all agreed, didn't we, Mom?" said Tristan, appealing for help.

Mrs. Turner looked up from the paper and sighed. " 'We all' did *not* include me. Tris, for heaven's sake, give the girls a chance."

"But they're just fooling around with it!"

"It so happens that we're making a TV commercial," said Berry.

Tristan was not impressed. "Exactly. You're just fooling around."

"And *you're* not going to fool around, is that what you're saying, Tristan?" said Terri. "Show us your Hollywood contract!"

"Yeah, Mr. Big Shot!" said Berry. "We won't stop a real pro. Just show us a contract, anytime, and you can have the camera."

Before Tristan could give them any more trouble, Mr. Turner arrived in the room. "I won't have my supper spoiled by silly arguments," he said. "Vanessa, why are you hanging around out in the hall?"

"Is that camera turned on? I'm not coming in if it's turned on," called Vanessa from outside the room.

"It's not. The coast is clear, love," said Mrs. Turner.

"You know what your trouble is, Vanessa?" said Mr. Turner as his stepdaughter entered. "You don't always act in a manner you can be proud of. Personally, I try my best at all times to behave in a civilized way. I can promise that you would never—I mean never—catch me doing something on camera that I'm ashamed of."

Neither Berry nor Terri paid much attention to what Mr. Turner was saying. Later, though, they both remembered his words.

Chapter Six

The next day, right after school, Berry and Terri began to plan their TV commercial. They sat together in their bedroom and dreamed up ideas. One of Berry's ideas sounded good to Terri, too.

"Video World movies are so good that when we play them, our cats always watch them, too," said Berry.

"Yeah!" said Terri. "That's great!"

So they started looking for the cats. They were big, fat cats. They were also a big, fat problem. They found Kablooey, Fooey, and Ratatouille quite quickly, asleep on different chairs and beds. They left them on Berry's bed and went off to search for Zooey and Ralph, the mother of all the other cats. They found neither of them. Meanwhile, Ratatouille—the Rat—wandered off again.

So they locked Kablooey and Fooey in their bedroom. Finally they found the Rat again out in the back hedge. But no matter how hard they looked, they could not find Zooey or Ralph.

Kablooey, meanwhile, decided to hide under Berry's bed in the farthest, grubbiest corner. After much yowling and hissing, Kablooey was dragged out, clinging for dear life to a sweatshirt Berry hadn't seen for months.

"Forget Ralph. Forget Zooey," said Terri as they carried the cats down the stairs to the den. But there they found Zooey asleep on the couch right in front of the TV. They had looked there at least ten times before. How exasperating!

They never did find Ralph.

"Let's set up the camera behind the TV set," said Berry. "We'll see all these cats looking toward the camera, watching something. 'What are these cats watching? Why, they're watching a Video World movie, that's what' is what we'll say on the videotape."

When the camera was set up, Terri looked through the viewer. Berry crouched behind the couch. She tried to stay out of sight while patting, heaving, and shoving four unhelpful cats into the kind of cute clump you always see on cat-food commercials.

It was hard to understand. The couch in front of the TV was the favorite napping place of every cat in the house. Suddenly, for no reason, it was absolutely the last place in the universe that any cat wanted to be. Time after time there were cat escapes, cat chases, and cat captures.

"There! Quick! Roll camera!" shouted Berry, somehow holding four cats together at once.

"No way!" complained Terri. "Two of them have their bottoms pointed at the TV. *That's* not going to convince people to rent from Video World."

Berry sighed and let go. The floor shook as four fat cats landed on it, one after another. They all ran for the door, which was closed. The cats lined up, one behind another. Four little heads bobbed back and forth as they looked at the girls, at the doorknob, and at the girls again.

One by one the two girls gathered up the animals and sat on the couch with their arms full of squirming cats, trying to think of a better idea.

Terri came up with it this time. The couch in the den was old and the fabric on its back was gaping at the bottom. Terri lay down on the floor behind the couch and carefully dug her arm farther and farther into the springs.

After a while, there was a small ripping noise. Terri's hand popped out between the cushions on the seat of the couch.

"Perfect!" said Berry. They traded places. Terri

held the cats in place on the seat of the couch. Berry lay down and thrust her arm through the hole. It emerged just behind the cats. With Terri's help, Berry closed her hand around four stringy little tails.

Immediately, the four annoyed cats stood up. They put their ears back. They growled. All of them started to claw and strain their way forward.

"Quick! I can hardly hold them!" shouted Berry. Terri rushed to the camera and started taping.

"It looks great! They're so anxious to see a Video World movie they're going to jump right into the TV!" At that moment, the tails slipped from Berry's hand and the cats shot off in all directions.

"How was it?" asked Berry.

Terri groaned. "You ruined it right at the end. If you're going to leave your arm hanging out like that, you might as well wave to the camera," she said. "Right now it's a commercial about a couch that eats kids."

One more time the cats were collected from their lineup at the door. One more time they were placed on the couch. One more time Berry lay down behind it, reached through, and trapped the cats' tails. But this time, after a few seconds of holding, she

shouted, "I'm letting go now!" As she did so, she jerked her arm back down between the cushions.

"Fabulous!" said Terri. "You should see it! It will win an award for sure!" Quickly they pulled the videotape out of the camera, put it into the VCR under the TV, and watched the very first shot of their very first commercial.

It was even better in color. There was a wide view of the cats lit only by the blue flicker from the TV set. Terri zoomed in to show them straining. The cats did look like they wanted to leap right into a Video World movie! Boom! They were gone. Quite fabulous!

"How long was it?" said Berry.

"Play it again," said Terri. This time she looked at her watch. A moment later Terri looked up and said, "Was that all?"

"How long?"

"Six seconds."

"Oh."

They were both silent for a moment, thinking about this new problem.

"We're going to have fifty-four more seconds looking at an empty couch," said Berry.

* * *

48

After supper, they helped their housekeeper wash the dishes and they explained the problem. "We've got about six seconds of exploding cats," said Terri. "Then, if you look really closely, you can see the couch eating Berry's hand."

"Some commercial," agreed Berry gloomily.

Dorothea was sympathetic. "Is there any way of stretching it? Maybe slowing down the picture in the camera?" asked Dorothea.

Terri went to look for the user's manual. Horror of horrors, she found Melissa reading it in the living room. "What are *you* doing with our manual?" said Terri, grabbing it.

"First Tristan, now Melissa!" she said when she got back to the kitchen.

"Just like vultures, aren't they?" said their housekeeper cheerfully. "Circling, circling, waiting to pick your bones."

"Well, they're not going to get us as long as our TV commercial is still alive," said Berry with determination.

Their commercial was still alive, but it was sickly. They found nothing in the manual to help them stretch six seconds of exploding cats. "What should we do, Dorothea?"

"Well, if you want my advice, what you shouldn't

do is use animals in your commercial," said Dorothea. "They're very hard to work with."

"Then we don't have anything!" moaned Berry.

"You've killed our poor little commercial," groaned Terri.

"What will we do now?" they wondered.

"Don't worry," said Dorothea. "You'll think of something."

Chapter Seven

Berry and Terri were sitting in their bedroom thinking up new ideas when Vanessa poked her head through the doorway. "Has anybody seen the manual?" she said.

"We're using it," said Terri. She snatched it up and began to read it.

"Why does everybody want it, anyway?" said Berry.

"Mom said anybody who wants to use the camera has to read the manual," explained Vanessa. "I'll get it later, don't worry."

"We won't," said Berry. But she *was* worried. The whole family was starting to grab for the camera.

"Hey!" said Terri, who was still studying the manual. "Did you notice this? We don't need a battery. There's an adaptor somewhere that lets us plug the camera into a wall outlet."

They searched through the camera packaging and found the adapter. Then they set the camera up in their bedroom and plugged it into an outlet. It worked.

Thanks to this little experiment, the camera captured the whole first scene of a disaster.

There was a knock on the door frame. It was Mr. Turner.

"Hi, Dad," said Terri as he came into the room.

"Excuse me," he said. "I've been hunting everywhere for an electrical extension cord. Your mother said she remembered seeing one hanging on the back of your closet door."

"Wait!" cried Berry. "You have to—" It was too late.

Berry had been doing her best to keep her half of the room as tidy as Mr. Turner liked to see it. The closet, which was out of sight, was the last part of the room that needed a little tidying. Terri had not really had a chance to move into it properly. Two cardboard boxes of her belongings were stacked on the closet floor.

On top of these were balanced several board games, books, and other difficult-to-organize things belonging to Berry. Terri had tried to stack them in a neat pile. It was a difficult thing to do because Berry used the closet as a clothes bin.

Above the board games, reaching to the height

of Mr. Turner's head, was a heap of clothing. Some of it was clean. Some of it was dirty. Berry had been planning to sort it one day soon.

It was all such a mess that Terri had more or less given up trying to tidy the closet. Now she had a guilty secret. One or two soiled T-shirts buried in the heap belonged to her.

Mr. Turner did not know that you needed to place your hand carefully against the tower as you opened the closet door. He found out the hard way.

The camera caught the entire horrible moment as the contents of the closet collapsed around Mr. Turner and into the room.

For a second he was speechless. But he quickly found his voice again. "Berry! Terri! This mess is beyond belief!" he said. "I'm holding you both responsible for cleaning it out immediately!"

"But most of it is Berry's," complained Terri.

"Aren't those yours?" said Mr. Turner, looking at the two toppled boxes on the floor of the cupboard.

"Yes, but I haven't had a chance—because Berry—"

Her father raised his hand to cut off her words. "I don't want to hear another word," he said. "You're both using the closet. You both sort it out.

And I want no more foolery with video cameras until you're finished."

Poor Berry and Terri! They were fresh out of ideas for a TV commercial. Their brothers and sisters were trying to get the camera away from them. And now they were forbidden to do anything but work to clean up a horrible mess.

Not only did the camera nicely capture the closet avalanche, it recorded the shouting match between Berry and Terri after Mr. Turner left the room.

Half an hour later Berry stamped downstairs. A gigantic bundle of laundry was piled high in her arms. Berry had tried to use the well-known sniff test to separate the dirty clothes from the clean ones. She was so mad that all she could smell was old socks. The only sensible thing to do was to stagger down to the basement and stuff everything, clean and dirty, into the washer.

Berry and Terri weren't much comfort to each other that night. They were still arguing long after the closet was tidy, long after the lights were out in the bedroom.

Later that night, while Terri snored, Berry did what she often did when things weren't going so well. She took her flashlight under the covers and wrote in her diary. It always made her feel a little better.

Ma chère Annamarie,

I am in despair. You never showed up! No calls either. Didn't you have my number? It's 619-555-9207. I'm still waiting, just in case.

Meanwhile, something incredible has happened! Terri and I have a video camera. I'll be able to send you a videotape and show you what I look like!

Dear Annamarie, we are identical twins, so I know you think you can see me by looking at yourself in the mirror. But you can't! All faces are lopsided! I learned that in school. When you look in the mirror, it puts the lop on the wrong side. Now, at last, you will be able to see your faraway twin with her lop on the right side!

Your true twin and loving step-triplet,
Beryllium

A voice outside the blankets made Berry jump. Guiltily, she snapped off the flashlight. But it was only Terri. She had woken up and was still grumbling. "Dad never gets angry as long as things stay neat and tidy," said Terri. "When are you going to catch onto that, Beryllium?"

Berry poked her head out from under the blankets. "How many times have you said that tonight? Please stop reminding me, Terri," she said into the darkness. "The closet's tidy now, so go to sleep. Anyway, your dad will be really happy in the morning when he sees all the laundry I've done."

Chapter Eight

Saturday morning began with a tremendous roar. It was so loud that everybody in the house sat straight up in their beds. All except Mr. Turner, who was getting ready for his most important day of work. He was down in the basement, roaring.

"What made that strange noise?" said Berry, looking sleepy-eyed toward her stepsister.

"*You* made that strange noise!" said an angry voice. There in the doorway stood Mr. Turner.

"Out of bed! Get that camera working! I'll give you something really important to videotape with your silly toy," he said. Berry and Terri sprang to obey him.

Berry was first to the camera. She switched it on and put her eye to the viewer. She found herself staring at a fistful of damp clothing being waved in front of the camera lens.

"What color do you see?" said Mr. Turner.

"The viewer only shows black and white," said Berry timidly.

"Black and white! Black and white! If only things *were* black and white. Open your other eye and tell me what color you see."

Berry opened her eye. "Pink," she said.

"Pink is correct!" shouted Mr. Turner. "I now own five expensive pink drip-dry shirts. And do you know why they're pink instead of white?"

"No," quavered Berry.

"Because you didn't look in the washing machine! You just opened it and stuffed in your load. My shirts were in there! You should have removed them and put them in the dryer. But oh, no! You didn't look!"

"Sorry," whispered Berry, hanging her head.

"You washed my shirts *again,* along with all your clothing, and in particular *these.*" Mr. Turner brandished the culprits in the air—a pair of damp red socks.

"But . . ." spluttered Berry. "But . . . those aren't my socks."

There was a long pause while Mr. Turner just stared at her. Then he and Berry both turned to look at Terri. "You mean to tell me that *your* socks have ruined my shirts, Terri?" His voice was no longer fierce. Instead, he sounded bewildered and hurt.

Terri was almost as neat as her father was. But lately, what with Berry throwing things all over the room, Terri had started to grow ever-so-slightly sloppy. She hung her head. She felt just like she had shot an arrow into her father's chest.

"Well!" said Mr. Turner as he tried to gather his thoughts. "Well! It seems you two have just been grasshoppers, in spite of all your promises. You both have chores to do in this household. You've been playing about and neglecting them."

"Okay, we won't do any more videotaping," said Berry miserably.

"Oh, no, you don't!" said Mr. Turner. He was over his shock and sounded stern once again. "That would be easy, wouldn't it? Blame the camera. The camera made us foolish and careless. Nonsense!"

Berry and Terri looked at each other, confused. What did Mr. Turner want them to say, or do?

"You must learn that the camera is just a tool that can be used foolishly or wisely," he continued. "So I want you to make *me* a videotape."

Now the two girls looked at each other in astonishment.

"Don't start smirking. It's going to be work, not

play. Forget about making let's-pretend TV commercials. I want you to begin at the beginning and videotape step-by-step how to completely clean and tidy your bedroom. And I mean *completely*."

Chapter Nine

"Here! Why all the long faces?" said Dorothea in her funny Australian accent at breakfast.

Mr. Turner was still grumpy. He had rewashed his shirts, but bleach hadn't completely solved the problem. Saturday was his biggest day at Movies, Movies, Movies. Thanks to Berry and Terri, he felt like a fool as he stamped off to work wearing a faintly pink shirt.

All the other kids in the family were grumpy because Terri had broken the bad news to them. "You can read the manual all you like. But you'll have to wait a lot longer to use the camera. Dad's making us do a big videotape on how to clean up our room."

Making the vultures grumpy was the only small enjoyment for Berry and Terri that morning. *They* weren't grumpy. They were both furious, but not with each other. They were mad at Mr. Turner.

"He left a wet load in the washing machine. That's against one of his own rules!" raged Terri when they returned to their room after breakfast.

"And we've been told over and over that we all have a right to privacy!" said Berry, just as mad. "He's supposed to warn us, or ask permission to look in the closet, not just yank the door open."

The more they talked it over, the more they believed that Mr. Turner had received just what he deserved. More closets should dump all over him. All his shirts should turn pink.

"But I guess there's nothing much we can do except make his dumb videotape," said Terri at last. She sighed.

"Well, I don't think we should stop making our TV commercial. He said not to make let's-pretend TV commercials, right?" said Berry.

"And we're *not* pretending," said Terri. "It's a real contest."

"We'll just have to do both," decided Berry. Terri agreed.

The trouble was, they were fresh out of good ideas for their commercial.

"Maybe we could show Izzy's goldfish watching video movies," said Terri. "And shoot the TV set right through the bowl!"

"Yawn," said Berry scornfully. "I've got a better idea." Because she was in a nasty mood, it turned out to be a nasty idea.

"But it's a *good* idea," said Terri after she heard it. "It would serve Dad right."

"And best of all, the pictures are easy," said Berry. "We only have to videotape three buildings—Movies, Movies, Movies, Video World, and our own house."

"Let's get started on the commercial while Dad's at work," said Terri. "We can do the room-cleaning stuff later, when he gets home."

Dorothea's plans for the morning did *not* include driving Berry and Terri and their camera anywhere. They had to really plead with their housekeeper before she agreed to take them to the Prospect Park Mall.

"I'll drop you off. You'll have to get a lift back with your dad, though, when he comes home for lunch," she warned.

That sounded a little dangerous. They didn't want to anger him again. But their mother had given them some money to buy some new videotapes. "We'll tell him that we came to the mall to buy tapes, and it will be the truth," said Terri.

Dorothea was a real nuisance that morning. She discovered that Berry and Terri planned to videotape Movies, Movies, Movies. But Dorothea would not let them wander around through the parked cars looking for the best camera position. Not without her, anyway.

She wasn't the best company. When she wasn't looking at her watch and fuming, she was shaking her head and saying, "I don't know. I don't see how you can put your dad's cinemas in a video rental commercial without him getting pretty upset." The two girls did their best to ignore Dorothea. Mr. Turner had made *them* upset. Fair was fair. It was his turn next.

Terri did a fine job of filming the cinema building. Slowly she zoomed in on the big sign above the entrance that showed which movies were playing at what times.

At last, they were finished. Dorothea, muttering, delivered them to their mother in her store. "We need to buy videotape, and since we were here, we thought it would be nice to take some videotape of Books & Bears," said Berry cheerfully.

The pair went back out into the mall. For a while, it really looked as if they were videotaping the outside of their mother's store. Only from a certain angle could you see that they were pointing the camera at the store next door and making a video-tape of Video World.

It was almost noon when they walked all the way back down the mall to Movies, Movies, Movies. Things were going smoothly. With any luck, they could tear Mr. Turner away from his work quickly and get back home to finish the commercial.

The doors to the cinemas weren't open yet so they tapped on the glass. One of the ushers let them into the plush red-carpeted lobby. "He's in number three, I think," said the usher.

The two girls, still lugging the camera and tripod, went down the lobby toward the fancy neon *3* glowing on the wall.

They parted the curtains and stepped into darkness. Right up at the front of the cinema was a single head watching a movie on the huge screen.

Berry and Terri were outraged.

"He's watching a movie!" said Terri.

"So *this* is what he does when he says he's coming to work early!" said Berry.

"Sssh," whispered Terri. "Let's videotape him! We'll show it to Mom and everybody. What a nerve!"

"But we can't wreck our commercial," warned

Berry. The videotape in the camera was all set to go for the last shot of the commercial, not for a spy video on their father. Fortunately, they had bought new tapes. Berry removed the old tape from the camera and replaced it with one of the new ones she was carrying.

As they set up the camera, there was a burst of familiar laughter from the front of the theater. "That's Dad all right," said Berry.

"You can't really tell with the camera, though," said Terri, her eye to the camera viewer as she taped. "I'm just seeing a little black head against the screen."

"Do you know, I even think he's eating popcorn!" said Berry in amazement. That was *really* goofing off.

"Let's sneak up the aisle and see if I can get his face," whispered Terri. They took the camera off the tripod.

The soundtrack of the movie was loud. It covered the noise they made as they crawled down the side aisle of the cinema. When they reached the row their father was sitting in, Terri eased the camera up over the arm of the chair.

"Great!" she breathed. She opened the lens of the camera as wide as it would go, to let in every bit of

light. Then she steadied the camera on the arm of the chair and zoomed slowly in on her father's face.

He was indeed eating popcorn. When he wasn't chuckling, that is. Mr. Turner was having a wonderful time all by himself.

When Terri was finished, they crawled back up the aisle and went back out into the lobby for a second. "Boy, is *he* ever going to get teased about this!" said Berry. She was delighted to find a real chance to get back at Mr. Turner for his recent meanness.

A moment later they poked their heads back into the cinema and shouted that they needed a lift home.

"Why are you dragging the camera around?" said Mr. Turner as they drove back to their house.

"We've got to do your room-cleaning video, remember?" said Terri. "If we leave the camera *anywhere* Tristan can find it, we'll never see it again." That answer seemed to satisfy Mr. Turner. His mood had improved since morning.

"Several of my staff complimented me on my pink shirt," he said with a small smile. "They think the color goes well with the blue jackets we all wear." Berry and Terri felt a little better when they heard this news.

Chapter Ten

Foolishly, the two girls did not wait till their father went back to work before taping the last shot of their commercial—their own house.

Mr. Turner almost ruined the shot by dashing out of the house and off to his car. Luckily, he didn't even notice them. Even more fortunately, the one-minute commercial ended just before he appeared on the videotape.

So now they had all the pictures they needed for their commercial. Next came the fun part—the sound effects.

Berry and Terri worked all afternoon in the basement making the soundtrack for their commercial. People upstairs frowned at one another as sudden shrieks of giggling came up through the floor. There were other, quieter noises, too. Some of them sounded very odd indeed.

The giggling was not meant to be part of the commercial, and one of the biggest problems Berry and

Terri faced was keeping their own laughter off the videotape.

At last the commercial was complete. They were tidying up the mess in the basement when Terri suddenly froze and cocked her ear to the ceiling.

"What's wrong?" said Berry.

"I thought I heard Dad's voice! But he wasn't coming home for supper."

"No," agreed Berry. But then she heard his voice, too. It was unmistakable.

"Oh, no!" said Terri. "He *is* back!"

"And he thinks we've been working on his video all afternoon," said Berry in a panic. "We've got to get up there and do something fast, otherwise we're going to be in big trouble again."

Would they even make it out of the basement without being caught? Luckily, Mr. Turner went back out to his car to collect something. In that brief moment, Berry and Terri scampered up to their bedroom.

Terri struggled to set up the camera. "I hear his feet on the stairs! Quick, Berry, get in front of the camera! Say something!" she said.

"What?" said Berry, looking frantically around the room. There must be a million things to say

70

about tidying up a room. But now that she was staring at the big fish-eye of the camera lens, Berry's mind was suddenly blank.

"You're the one with all the ideas! Start talking! Now!" hissed Terri. The footsteps were on the landing now, growing louder.

"Well, um, like, um, er—" Berry's eyes darted in all directions. "Stuffed toys!"

She grabbed a teddy bear as though it had come to save her from drowning. "You, er, tidy stuffed toys, by, uh . . . size!" She dropped the teddy bear and grabbed her largest doll. "Big, like this . . . here, maybe." She placed it carefully at one end of Terri's tidy dresser. "And small, er . . . at the other end."

Berry looked so uncomfortable that Terri couldn't bear to watch. She closed her eyes. Terri could almost hear her father's teeth grinding in the doorway behind her.

"And in the middle, um . . . middle-size!" said Berry. She suddenly shot off camera, and reappeared with an armload of other stuffed toys. Grinning foolishly at the camera, she fumbled them into a line with the tallest on the left and shortest on the right.

"Or you could, um, use color!" said Berry. Her face was shiny now. She was beginning to sweat.

"Aaaah . . . Buuuh . . . Brown! Starting with brown! No, brrr, bllluh. No, blue! But . . . unh. There isn't anything blue! So brown!"

She picked up two teddy bears, then fumbled them both onto the floor. Berry's performance was so bad that Terri wanted to join the bears and crawl under the rug, too.

"Oh, Berry, Berry, Berry!" groaned Mr. Turner in the doorway. "This isn't important! This isn't planned! What have you girls been *doing*?" They were in trouble again, unless—

Of all the millions and billions of things to say, only one thing could have saved them. And Terri just happened to say that one thing. "Gee, Dad, I'm afraid we're not very good actors. We were hoping you could help us."

Mr. Turner gave an exhausted sigh and shook his head wearily. "Of all the things to hear after a hard day's work!" he said. Berry and Terri believed completely that Mr. Turner wanted to do anything but help them make their video. But they were wrong.

Their father had a deep, dark secret—one he would never have admitted to anyone. Of all the people in their whole scrambled-up household, Mr. Turner itched more than anybody to get his hands on the camera! Of course, he had only been asked to help with the acting, but . . .

He sighed again wearily. "Well, I suppose I might be able to spare a *little* time."

A little time stretched into a long time. Mr. Turner wasn't camera-shy. He gave exactly the same kind of lecture, on or off camera. This was just what a very serious room-tidying video needed.

The girls hardly noticed how often Mr. Turner found excuses to come and check the view through the camera or to test little zooms in and out. Mr. Turner was having fun.

When supper was announced, Mr. Turner shouted through the closed door of the bedroom. "Ants working! Do not disturb!" he said.

Hot dogs for three were sent up on a tray. Berry, Terri, and Mr. Turner worked hard for four hours that Saturday night. To the astonishment of the two girls, they wound up having a wonderful time.

It was nine o'clock that evening before they finished their "Truly Excellent How-To-Tidy-A-Room Video." And with their father's help, Berry and Terri found it easy to get the whole family together for the first showing.

He just ordered everybody to be there. And they

were! Everybody except Dorothea. She said she would only watch a video about housekeeping during her normal housekeeping hours.

And what were the comments?

"Oh, no! Dad's using his army voice," whispered Paul to Tristan. "Do we all have to stand at attention while we watch?"

"I never knew one man could say so much about how to fold socks," said Mrs. Turner.

"I never knew my father was such a ham!" whispered Melissa to Izzy.

"If Berry and Terri are straightening that blanket, who's running the camera?" said Vanessa.

"Nobody," said Mr. Turner.

"That's not true! Look! Look! It's zooming!" said Izzy.

"It's Dad! Dad's running the camera! How come Dad suddenly gets to play with the camera? It's not fair to the rest of us!" complained Melissa.

"Be quiet, everyone," said Mr. Turner. "Pay attention. You might learn something."

And what was the verdict?

"It's the single most boring half-hour of television I've ever watched in my life!" said Paul. Mrs. Turner, Vanessa, Tristan, Melissa, and Izzy agreed with every word.

"Well made! Well acted! Brilliant!" said Mr. Turner. Berry and Terri agreed with every word.

They had enjoyed themselves so much with their father that they were beginning to feel terribly guilty about the TV commercial they had just finished. But what should they do about it?

In the end, they asked Dorothea. They dragged her out of her room over the garage and sat her in front of the TV.

"What do you think?" they asked anxiously after they played the videotape.

"No!" said Dorothea firmly. "Absolutely not! You *cannot* enter that video in a contest."

"Are you *sure?*" said Berry.

"You look at it again yourselves. You tell me what's wrong with it."

The first picture was a shot of Mr. Turner's new six-plex cinema. Meanwhile, strange sticky noises came from the TV.

Now Berry's voice was on the videotape. "Do you recognize that sound?" she said. "It's the sound of your feet sticking to all the icky old butter on the floor of a movie cinema."

The scene didn't change but the sound did. Suddenly there was a *kersploosh*ing, rattling noise. "That's the sound a drink makes when you kick it

75

over in the dark while you're looking for your seat," said Berry.

Next, there was a wet *splutt*ing sound. "And that's the sound you hear when you sit on an old ice-cream bar. Those are all sounds you can expect when you watch a movie at a cinema."

The scene changed to show Video World. "If you want to stay clean, and really enjoy watching a movie, come to Video World," said Berry's voice.

The last scene was the front of the Turner house. "Rent a movie and take it to the very best cinema of all—your own house. You can watch it from your favorite chair, and you won't ever hear—*kersploosh, splutt.*"

As usual, the two girls thought it was hilarious and giggled all the way through the commercial. But when it was over, Dorothea faced them, scowling. "Well?" she said.

"Dad would be pretty mad," admitted Berry.

"*Pretty* mad!" said Dorothea. "Are you trying to ruin his business? What got into your heads, anyway?"

"We were angry with him," said Terri.

"And why is he running out of the house at the end of the commercial, anyway?" said Dorothea.

"We were going to cut that part off," said Berry.

"Well, don't bother," said Dorothea. "It shows exactly what your father will probably do if you give that commercial to Video World. He'll leave home. For good! I'll have to leave, too. After all, I helped you make it."

The smiles faded on Berry's and Terri's faces. They looked at each other miserably. Then they were distracted by a hammering on the door of the den.

"Mom says it's past your bedtime," called Izzy. When the door opened, Tristan was standing there, too.

"She also says she wants you to give me a turn on the camera tomorrow unless you can come up with something to make her change her mind. So *have* you got anything to show her to change her mind?" said Tristan.

Berry and Terri shook their heads.

"It looks like the end of the TV commercial contest," said Berry as they got ready for bed.

"No way. Dad always says, 'When the going gets tough, the tough get going,'" said Terri. "So let's get going."

Chapter Eleven

It was Sunday morning. The tough were not going at all. Their bedroom door was still closed. The tough were sleeping in after a late night. After much thought, Berry and Terri had come up with a really *sensational* idea for a TV commercial. Not only that, they had a fiendishly clever plan to keep Tristan from stealing the camera.

At ten o'clock, they awoke and dressed quickly. They found Tristan lying on his bed studying *their* video-camera manual. He snapped his fingers impatiently when he saw them. "Camera, please," he said.

The two girls piled onto the bed with him and overwhelmed him with hugs and kisses.

"Oh, Tris, you're our favorite brother and the cleverest person in the whole family," said Berry.

"We desperately need your help," said Terri.

"Uh-oh," said Tristan. Tristan was a sucker for people who needed help. He knew it, too.

The girls swore Tristan to secrecy. They told him

all their plans. He did his best to pretend that he wasn't excited, but they knew he was.

"There's a price for this," he said, trying to look hard and mean.

"We know. You get to use the camera next, right?" said Terri.

"How *did* you guess?" said Tristan, grinning.

It wasn't long before Berry and Terri knew they had made the right decision. Tristan *loved* their idea. And more than anything else in the world he *loved* to fiddle and play with wires and switches and connectors.

Working with Tristan was like sitting in a box of lighted fireworks. There were sudden sparks and explosions that made them jump.

"Right!" He would pop up from behind the TV, hair flying, eyes wild.

"Good!" He would shoot back down again, a wire in his hand.

"Aha!" Here he was connecting something to something else.

"Perfect!" There he was connecting that something else to the camera.

Tristan asked Dorothea to drive him fifteen miles away to a huge discount video mart. It was open on Sundays. There he spent thirty-five dollars of his own money on special cables and other bits and pieces.

He wouldn't hear of being paid back. "I'll need them for what I want to do with the camera, anyway," he said to his two young sisters.

It was Tristan who managed the absolutely impossible. He talked their father out of watching a San Diego Chargers football game on TV. It was Tristan who figured out how to lock the door of the den so that nobody could get in and interrupt their project.

Berry and Terri had already shot every inch of videotape they needed. By two in the afternoon, Tristan had helped them play back pieces of six different videotapes on the VCR under the television. These were all recorded again in the camera onto a brand-new videotape. Together the scenes added up to exactly one minute. The nicest thing of all about Tristan was that he did exactly what they asked. "You tell me. I'll just be the technician. You be the artists," he insisted. Tristan loved being a technician.

The soundtrack turned out to be more complicated than putting the picture together. But with Tristan's help they added Berry's commentary to other voices and sounds on the tape.

Finally, just before supper, they sat back and watched the complete commercial from start to finish.

There was a long silence when the commercial was over.

"What do you think, Tris?" asked Berry at last. She sounded worried.

"I think it's *good,*" he said. He sounded like he meant it.

"About Dad, though. He's really the most important part of the commercial, isn't he?" Berry had suddenly remembered Mr. Turner's words of a few days ago. About how nobody likes to be embarrassed in public. Were they going to embarrass their father?

They discussed it. "Let's ask Dorothea," said Tristan. So they did.

Dorothea came and watched. This time she seemed really pleased. *"Very* impressive, girls. I'm proud of you."

"But what about Dad?"

Dorothea frowned and thought. At last she said, "Well, you're certainly not ruining his business with this commercial. As for embarrassing him, you can't really do that."

"Why?"

"Because nobody can use those pictures of your father in public without his permission." Dorothea was really a folksinger, and only a part-time housekeeper. She knew about that kind of thing.

"Why don't you kids do this?" she said. "Enter the contest. If you don't win, well, they won't show the commercial anywhere, so it doesn't matter. If you do win something, and they want to show it in public—well, you'll have to ask your father at that time. He'll be able to say no if he wants to."

"Okay," agreed Terri. "So we just cross our fingers and hope that we lose."

Dorothea drove their commercial to Video World the next day.

Terri did not keep her fingers crossed, though. She didn't want to lose.

Chapter Twelve

The phone call came in the evening, three days later.

Mrs. Turner came into the living room, where half the family was trying to read while the other half played a loud game of Monopoly. "Some strange man is asking to talk to either Berry or Terri Turner," she said with a slight frown.

"Probably just a rug-cleaning salesperson," said Mr. Turner, not looking up from his book.

It wasn't. When Berry and Terri crept into the living room they looked pale, and their voices were a little shaky. "We should have *wished* a little harder that we would lose," whispered Terri.

"Yeah, sure!" whispered Berry. She grinned at Terri. Terri grinned back.

"What do we do now?" said Berry.

Their mother noticed them standing in the doorway. "How can two people look so excited and so worried at the same time?" she said.

"Um," said Berry. There was no way around it.

They would have to explain, difficult as it might be. "Well, remember when you all thought we were playing at making TV commercials?" Berry's voice was so wobbly that the entire family looked up.

"We weren't playing. We entered a TV-commercial contest. A real one," said Terri.

"You didn't!" said the surprised Mrs. Turner.

"We did," said Berry. "And that man was calling to tell us we've won a prize."

"No!" said Mr. Turner, putting down his book. "You mean my two grasshoppers have been ants in disguise all along?"

Berry and Terri nodded happily. Mr. Turner stood and embraced them both.

"Come on! Don't let them sucker you in, Dad. They're kidding," scoffed Melissa.

"Yeah!" agreed Izzy.

"No, it *is* true," said Tristan. "I helped them. Just a little." His brother and sisters looked at him in surprise. Tristan looked pleased, too.

"So what did you win, then? The booby prize?" said Izzy.

"We really don't know, Izzy," said Berry. "They say we've won *something* and they've asked if we can come to the awards ceremony. It's going to be at the San Diego Convention Center."

"Well, of *course* you can go. I'll be proud to drive you!" said Mr. Turner.

"We'll *all* go," said Mrs. Turner.

Berry and Terri looked at each other. The time had come. They had to say it.

"There *is* a little problem, though," said Berry. "They might want to show the video to an audience there. So we have to make sure that we have everybody's permission who's in it."

"Well, you can have *my* permission," said Melissa.

"Sorry, Melissa, you're not in it," said Berry.

"Well, who *is* then?" said Mr. Turner, looking puzzled.

"You," said Terri.

"Me?" said Mr. Turner. Suddenly he didn't look pleased. "Wait a minute now. How did that happen? Exactly what *is* this contest, anyway?"

"Well . . ." said Berry. She took a deep breath. "It's just Video World's Second Annual TV-Commercial Contest." She did her best to mumble the words together, as though she could somehow hide the truth. It was no use.

"Video World! The video rental place? I'm starring in a commercial for *video rentals*?" said Mr.

Turner. His voice was still quiet, but his face was growing fierce and red.

"It's okay, Dad! It's okay," said Terri hastily. "You only have to say no and they won't show it."

"Good!" said Mr. Turner.

"But will you win anything then?" asked their mother.

"No. But that doesn't matter," said Berry. "Really."

"Oh, for heaven's sake!" said Mr. Turner, quite furious. He was feeling cornered. He didn't want his daughters to lose out, but he also didn't want to be part of a Video World TV commercial, homemade or not. "How did you *ever* imagine I'd agree to let you use videotape of me?"

"Well," said Berry, "you *did* say the other day that you would never mind being videotaped, because you were never ashamed of anything you did."

"Well, now. That was a very careless thing of you to say, dear," said Mrs. Turner.

"I beg your pardon?" said Mr. Turner coldly.

"Well, you shouldn't say things you don't mean," said his wife.

"I *never* say things I don't mean," said Mr. Turner fiercely.

"Then I guess you don't mind appearing in a videotape the girls made?" said Mrs. Turner with a cheerful smile.

Mr. Turner was trapped, and he knew it. When he finally muttered, "Well, at least I might have been shown it first!" Berry and Terri knew they had won.

"Don't worry, Dad. You might even like it," said Terri.

Chapter Thirteen

The entire gigantic convention center had been taken over by an electronics show. "Video 2000" had come to San Diego. Crowds of people pushed their way past booths crammed with all the latest video recorders and video cameras.

It took the Turner family a long time to find the auditorium, partly because Tristan and Dorothea wanted to stop and play with every shiny electronic toy they saw. Everyone was having a good time except Mr. Turner. Berry and Terri walked with him, each holding one of his hands to give him as much support and comfort as possible.

Mr. Turner nearly fainted when he saw the sign outside the auditorium.

San Diego Area Video Rental Association
presents
THE SECOND ANNUAL VIDEO WORLD
TV COMMERCIAL AWARDS

*   *   *

"It's *them,*" he whispered. "They're the *enemy.* I can't go in there!"

"Nonsense. You're being silly, Nicholas," said his wife. "Anyway, they'll never know who you are." Berry and Terri looked at each other uncomfortably. They wished their mother hadn't said that.

There was quite a crowd in the auditorium. Many people had stopped to rest their weary feet. The Turners at last found ten seats together and sat down. Up on the platform at the front, several men in suits stood before a huge white screen.

"We'll get the runner-up prize," whispered Berry to Terri.

But they didn't. The hall fell silent as one by one the awards were called out in two categories—under-eighteen, and under-thirteen.

Runners-up in both categories were named. None of the names was Turner. As the audience applauded, the winners went to receive their prizes. The screen behind the platform stayed blank.

"We'll get third prize, then," whispered Terri. Nope. Names were called for third prizes. The Turner name was not among them, either.

"Wow! Second prize!" whispered Berry, hardly

able to believe it. And, indeed, the name "Turner" did ring out from the public-address system.

Berry and Terri were both half standing when their mother pulled them down. Neither of them was sixteen. Nor were they called Simon and John.

The Turner brothers collected their second prize in the under-eighteen category. Berry and Terri were stunned. There were only the first prizes and the grand prize left.

"Ladies and gentlemen, first prize in the under-thirteen category . . . Berry and Terri Turner!" Berry and Terri floated to their feet as if they were in a dream. They pushed their way past their astonished brothers and sisters.

Inside each of them, two invisible nine-year-olds were poking their fingers at the noses of each brother and sister and saying, "Ha! See!"

Nobody was saying "Ha!" to Tristan, though. Berry caught his hand and tried to drag him with them. He hung back. "It was all your idea," he said as he pried his hand loose. Then Berry and Terri were all alone, walking up the aisle to the platform as the crowd applauded.

After shaking hands with five smiling men, they were guided to one side of the platform. The lights dimmed. And there, huge above their heads on the big screen, was their very own commercial.

It began with Berry standing in their bedroom. Now her voice boomed out across the auditorium. "I'm Berry. I'm kind of messy." As she spoke, her father stepped into view and opened the closet door. The auditorium roared with laughter as he was hit by an avalanche of junk.

"My father thinks messiness is a disease," said Berry's voice. "He thinks my sister Terri is catching it from me." The scene shifted to Mr. Turner, shaking pink shirts and wet socks at Terri.

"You mean to tell me that *your* socks have ruined my shirts, Terri?" said the big-screen Mr. Turner. The audience laughed again. The real Mr. Turner shrank down and covered his eyes.

"Our dad has to work hard to teach us how to be tidy," said Berry. The camera changed to Mr. Turner, kneeling at the corner of Terri's bed.

"Hospital corners!" barked Mr. Turner in his army voice. "Left hand lifts the sheet, so. Right hand tucks, now fold down, pull tight, and tuck." As he spoke, Mr. Turner demonstrated a neat hospital corner on the bedsheet.

"Shirts! Fold, so. Left arm, right arm, over . . ."

The camera showed Mr. Turner demonstrating how to fold a shirt.

"We make our dad so tired it's not surprising he sometimes runs away to work, just so he can relax," said Berry's voice. Mr. Turner ran from the house to his car.

Next, the camera cut to Movies, Movies, Movies. "Our dad has one of the neatest jobs in the world," said Berry. "He's the manager of the new cinemas at the Prospect Park Mall. If our dad wants to watch a movie, he can do it the same time as everybody else, but he doesn't have to pay. Great, eh?" The camera zoomed in on the big sign over the entrance that showed the movies and the times they were playing.

"But if we've made him really tired, and he wants to sneak off in the morning, or the middle of the night even, he's *especially* lucky." Now the camera showed one head watching a movie in an empty theater, right up at the front. "He can watch his very own movie the very best way, on a big screen, *any* time he wants." There was Terri's best sneaky camera shot as she slowly zoomed in on her dad, chuckling and munching away, watching the film all by himself. "He even gets to eat free popcorn!

"Most people aren't as lucky as my dad. They

don't own their own cinemas." Now the picture cut to a view of the Video World store. "But if your kids make you tired, and you need to relax early in the morning, or even in the middle of the night, you *can* do it! How? Just rent a movie videotape from the very best movie renters, Video World." The picture faded to black.

Then the lights were on again in the auditorium and the audience was applauding loudly. Berry and Terri stood there, uncomfortable but delighted. Out in the audience a bewildered Mr. Turner said, "Gosh, was that a commercial for Video World, or was it a commercial for my cinemas?"

"I really think it was both, dear," said Mrs. Turner happily.

Meanwhile, up on the stage, Berry and Terri were starting to leave. "No, don't go," whispered the man next to them. Berry looked at Terri. Surely they hadn't won the grand prize, too?

Two tall, serious-looking seventeen-year-old girls were called next to receive the first prize in the under-eighteen category.

The lights dimmed and Berry and Terri watched the video in amazement. It was incredible! It was all animation. Videotape boxes did a dance in time to music. This commercial looked like it belonged on *real* TV.

After the applause died down, two nine-year-olds and two seventeen-year-olds stood nervously side by side as one of the men announced the grand prize.

Berry and Terri didn't win. The two older girls gave tiny smiles of triumph as their names were called, and a brand-new video camera was presented to them.

"They probably need it. We don't," whispered Berry to Terri.

Then they smiled bravely and shook hands with the older girls. Berry had to say exactly what she felt. "That was awesome," she said. The faces of the two older girls suddenly broke into wide smiles.

"Did you really think so?" one of them said.

"Gosh, your *idea* was so good," said the other. "When we saw your commercial, we thought you'd win the grand prize for sure!" A moment later the four girls were chattering to one another right there on the stage. They were four video-makers holding their own private celebration party.

The audience began to titter, and at last the master of ceremonies interrupted. "I asked our two younger competitors to stay on the stage because

I think we'd all like to meet their dad. I understand he is here with us, right?" Berry nodded.

Mr. Turner hunched down in his seat. It was no good, though. His wife forced him to stand and acknowledge the applause of the audience.

"Let's hear it for a good sport! Come on up here, Mr. Turner!" called the master of ceremonies. Looking stiff and awkward, Mr. Turner joined his daughters on the stage.

"I know that I, as president of Video World, owe my thanks to Mr. Turner. And I hope he has reminded our entire association of video renters that we are in a great partnership with cinemas.

"The dollars *they* earn and the dollars *we* earn together make it possible for our American movie industry to be the greatest in the world," he continued. "Thanks for reminding us of that partnership, Mr. Turner!" Strong applause from the audience astonished and pleased Mr. Turner.

"And I don't mind telling you, Mr. Turner, that we at Video World just *loved* your daughters' commercial. So much so we'd like to talk to you about getting together and making it again, professionally. I think it could be a great advertisement for *your* cinemas and *our* video stores."

After more applause, the Turners were allowed

to return to their seats. "Did we do okay, Dad?" whispered Berry as they walked down the aisle.

She knew what the answer was, really. So it served her right, what happened next. Mr. Turner stopped in the middle of the aisle. In front of the entire audience, he picked up first Berry and then Terri and give them huge, sloppy kisses. The audience loved it. Berry and Terri didn't like it at all.

It was only later, as they were fighting their way out of the convention center, that Mr. Turner asked, "So what did you win? I never did find out, kids."

"Two free movie rentals a week for a whole year," said Terri proudly. *"Free,"* she said again, in case he hadn't heard the first time.

"What? Free? *A hundred and four* free movies? Wow! You can't find a bargain better than that!" said Mr. Turner, his eyes bright. Terri dug Berry in the ribs with her elbow.

The entire family spent the evening clustered around the couch in the den. "I'm afraid there is just a *little* bad news for Berry and Terri today," said Mrs. Turner.

"Sssh," said everybody.

"I'm taking back your birthday present."

"Sssh," said everybody.

"Your video camera, remember?"

"Yeah, thanks, Mom," said Berry, her eyes on the TV.

"I'm going to give it to the *entire* family instead. I think a point has been made. Berry and Terri deserve to use it as much as anybody. In fact, you'll all have to work pretty hard to use the camera as well as they did. Of course, Berry and Terri, this means you'll both have to get other presents on your birthday."

"Sssh," said everybody. They were just halfway through the first of one hundred and four free rentals. Nobody likes people talking in the middle of movies, so Mrs. Turner shrugged and watched, too.

Late that night, when everyone was in bed, Terri crept downstairs and quietly closed the door to the den. She shoveled a few hundred pounds of cat off the couch and put a videotape into the VCR. She pressed PLAY and settled back to watch.

There on the screen was her almost-twin stepsister. Berry looked awkward. Funny how she got shy when the camera pointed at her. What was even funnier was Berry's little speech. Funny-weird.

"Masher Annamarie," heard Terri. "Sorry about the scratching and blinking. It didn't work after all. But this video camera does. It's taken me this long to get it away from Terri. Just because her hands are steadier than mine, she thinks she's the only one who can use it.

"Don't worry, I've hidden this tape where she'll never find it in a million years. So this is your chance to see what I look like." Berry went on and on. Terri grew more and more puzzled.

After this very odd scene ended, Terri was about to remove the videotape when an even stranger scene began.

It was Berry again, although somehow it didn't quite look like her. She was wearing a beret and looked like she had rouge on her cheeks. This almost-Berry wasn't camera-shy at all. She waved her arms all over the place and talked in a funny accent.

"Allo, Berree! Eet ees me, Annamarie. Ah was so appy to see eeyou. Eeyou look almos lak me. Ownlee more beautifool." Strangest of all, this creature then babbled on and on about the wonderful weather in Paris, France.

Terri's frown grew deeper and deeper. She was obviously sharing a room with a complete fruitcake.

It's where everything happens!
by Ann Hodgman

___#1: NIGHT OF A THOUSAND PIZZAS 0-425-12091-0/$2.75

It all started with the school lunchroom's brand new, computerized pizza maker. Instead of one-hundred pizzas, the cook accidentally programmed it to make one thousand! What can the kids do? Have you ever tried to get rid of a thousand extra-large pizzas?

___#2: FROG PUNCH 0-425-12092-9/$2.75

This time the principal has gone too far. Ballroom dancing lessons. UGH! Even worse, he's planned a formal dance. Now the sixth grade is determined to fight back. When they unleash their secret weapon in the lunchroom, things will go completely bonkers!

___#3: THE COOKIE CAPER 0-425-12132-1/$2.75

The kids want to sell their baked cookies to raise money for the class treasury. But where will they find a kitchen big enough? The lunchroom! The cookies turn out to be so amazing the kids at Hollis get to be on TV, but the baking business turns out to be more than *anybody* needed!

___#4: THE FRENCH FRY ALIENS
0-425-12170-4/$2.75

It's going to be super scary when the kids give their performance of the class play. Especially since the sixth grade's all-new *Peter Pan* looks like it may turn into The French Fry Aliens—an interplanetary mess!

One day Allie, Rosie, Becky and Julie saved a birthday party from becoming a complete disaster. The next day, the four best friends are running their own business...

Don't miss these Party Line Adventures!

by Carrie Austen

___#1: ALLIE'S WILD SURPRISE 0-425-12047-3/$2.75
Allie's favorite rock star is in town, but how will she get the money for a concert ticket? When the clown hired for her little brother's birthday party is a no-show, Allie finds her miracle! Before you can say "make a wish," the girls are in the party business--having fun and getting paid for it! Can The Party Line make Allie's rock concert a dream come true?

___#2: JULIE'S BOY PROBLEM 0-425-12048-1/$2.75
It's hard to get a romance going with the cute Mark Harris when his best friend, Casey Wyatt, is an obnoxious girl-hater. Then, in the misunderstanding of the century, The Party Line gets hired to give a party for Casey. When Casey finds out, it's all-out war.

___#3: BECKY'S SUPER SECRET   0-425-12131-3/$2.75
Becky is putting together a top secret mystery party and she'll need her three best friends to help her do it in style. The only problem is: Becky hasn't exactly told them yet that they're going to help. Can Becky pull off the surprise party of the year?

___#4: ROSIE'S POPULARITY PLAN   0-425-12169-0/$2.75
It's just Rosie's luck to get paired with Jennifer--the weird new girl--for an English project. Next, Jennifer's mom thinks it would be a great idea if The Party Line threw a birthday party for Jennifer. The rest of the girls will need some serious convincing!